When Sophie Gets Angry— Really, Really Angry...

BY MOLLY BANG

SCHOLASTIC INC.

New York   Toronto   London   Auckland   Sydney
Mexico City   New Delhi   Hong Kong

Sophie
was busy
playing
when...

MY TURN

...her sister grabbed Gorilla.

"No!" said Sophie.
"Yes!" said her mother.
"It is her turn now,
Sophie."

As her sister
snatched Gorilla
away...

...Sophie
fell over
the truck.

Oh,
is Sophie
ever angry
now!

She kicks. She screams.
She wants to smash the
world to smithereens.

She
roars
a red,
red roar.

Sophie is a volcano,
ready to explode.

And when Sophie
gets angry—
really, really angry...

...she runs!

She runs and runs
and runs until she
can't run anymore.

Then,
for a little while,
she cries.

Tweet

Now she sees the rocks,
the trees and ferns.
She hears a bird.

She comes to the
old beech tree.
She climbs.

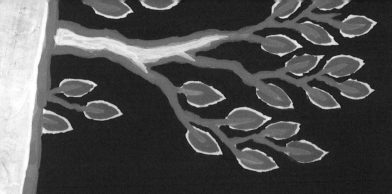

She feels the breeze
blow her hair.
She watches the water
and the waves.

The wide world
comforts her.

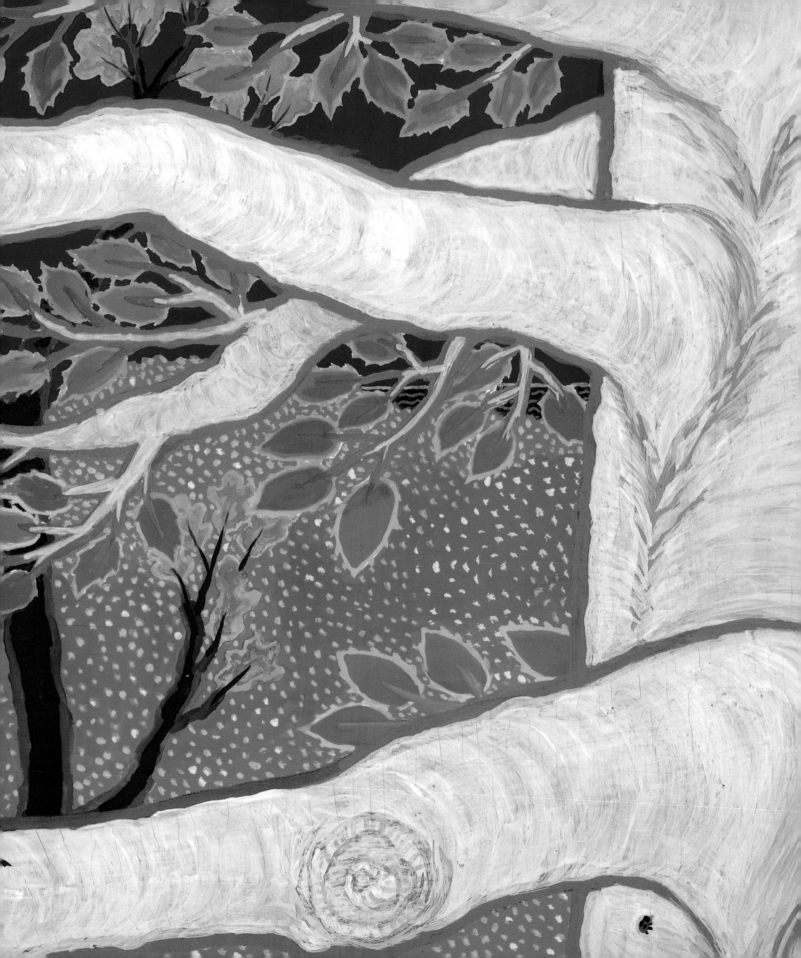

Sophie feels better now. She climbs back down...

...and heads for home.

i'm HOMe

The house is warm and smells good.
Everyone is glad she's home.

And Sophie
isn't angry
anymore.

PURR

To all children, and to all moms and dads,
grandmothers and grandfathers, aunts and uncles and friends,
who ever get angry — even once.
M. B.

When Sophie gets angry, she runs out and
climbs her favorite tree.
Different people handle anger in different ways.

What do you do when you get angry?

No part of this publication may be reproduced in whole or in part, or
stored in a retrieval system, or transmitted in any form or by any
means, electronic, mechanical, photocopying, recording, or otherwise,
without written permission of the publisher.
For information regarding permission, please write to:
Permissions Department, Scholastic Inc.,
555 Broadway, New York, NY 10012.

This book was originally published in hardcover
by the Blue Sky Press in 1999.

ISBN 0-439-23326-7

Copyright © 1999 by Molly Bang
All rights reserved.
Published by Scholastic Inc.
SCHOLASTIC and associated logos are trademarks and/or
registered trademarks of Scholastic Inc.

12 11 10 9 8 7 6 5 4 3 2 1   0 1 2 3 4 5/0

Printed in the United States of America

First Scholastic paper-over-board printing, September 2000